Sam the Superhero and His Super Life

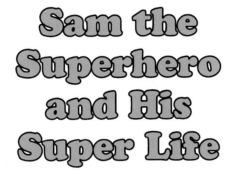

Written by Kathryn F. Pearson
& James T. Pearson
Illustrated by Lauren Jezierski

This is **Sam**. Sam lives with his grandparents – Grandma Lucy and Grandpa Dan. Sam loves to run around, play, and listen to Grandpa Dan read to him.

Sam and Grandpa Dan often go to the park to play tag, hide-and-seek, or his favorite, baseball. Sam loves baseball.

If Sam's grandparents can't play with him, Sam plays with his favorite stuffed dog named **Hercules**. Sam brings Hercules everywhere, even to school. Sam and Hercules have a lot of fun together. Hercules is also there to comfort Sam whenever Sam is upset.

Sam is a happy child, mostly. He loves his family but sometimes has trouble at school. There are times when Sam feels like the other kids in school don't understand him. When he was little Sam felt like he had a ton of friends. He loved playing with his classmates at recess, giving everyone hugs. They all hugged him back. Now when Sam tries to hug his classmates, they tell him he is *"too rough"*, and they shy away. Sam does not understand why.

Sam is also noticing now that he has more trouble in class than most of his classmates. When the teacher asks a question, Sam takes a little longer than the other kids to raise his hand, *even* when he knows the answer.

When the teacher asks Sam to write on the board, he finds it difficult to hold the marker. Sam doesn't know why this happens, and it makes him feel **angry** and **sad**.

In class there can be lot of noise and the lights can be very bright. This can make Sam's stomach **hurt**.

Loud noises especially feel painful in his stomach and his head. Sam feels like he **cannot even think** when this happens. There are days when distractions like these are too **overwhelming** for Sam, and it makes him upset.

When Sam gets upset like this, the Teacher, Mr. Rolph, helps Sam to a **quiet place** where he can **calm down**. Sam is happy that he brings Hercules with him to school during times like this.

When school is over, he gets to stay for aftercare while he waits for Grandpa Dan to pick him up.

Sam loves aftercare because it is the time when Sam gets to run fast and play with Hercules without bothering anyone.

One day at aftercare, Sam noticed that his classmates were picking teams. They had four cones shaped in a diamond on the field...they were going to play **baseball!**

Sam ran to the field quickly so he could be picked for a team and waited excitedly for his name to be called. Sam knew he would be picked – he is so fast!

The captains, Olivia and Brady, began picking teams. One by one all the student's names were called, until Sam was the only kid left. The teams began to walk over to the field.

Sam's name did not get called. Sam's smile left his face. "But I'm still here! **Whose team will I be on?**" he asked. Olivia and Brady turned around. "You can't play Sam" said Olivia.

Before Sam could say anything else, they turned away and walked to their teams. At that moment Sam felt what Grandpa Dan called "big feelings".

All at once his stomach hurt, he clenched his fists, and he started to cry. He walked over to the bench near the field and sat with Hercules **watching** the other kids start the baseball game without him. Grandpa Dan arrived after the first inning and sat down next to Sam.

"Hey there Little One, how was your day?" *"**Terrible**. The kids don't want to play with me." "Well that's not very nice. Do you want to go over and try again?" "No." replied Sam.

"It doesn't matter. If they don't want me to play with them then I won't bother asking anymore." Sam sighed and looked down.

"No one will be my friend."

"So, you're going to give up on having friends for the rest of your life then, Little One?" asked Grandpa Dan. "Yes. I don't need friends."

"Sam," Grandpa Dan said as he put an arm around Sam "let's go home. I've got something I want to show you."

When they got home, Grandpa Dan led Sam into the living room and told him to sit on the couch. Sam watched as Grandpa Dan pulled a teal box from the top shelf of the bookcase. Sam noticed that the shoebox had the word *"Sam"* written in gold letters on the top.

Grandpa joined Sam on the couch.

"I know you never want to make friends again, but you see, I think that's too easy." *Easy?* " asked Sam. How could ignoring people be "easy?" Sam thought to himself. They're all so loud!

"You see, anyone can refuse to be nice to others, never make friends, and spend the rest of their life alone. But, on the other hand," Grandpa Dan paused, looking at Sam in the eyes, "It takes a very strong person to stand up for themselves when others are being mean to them, and to reach out to new friends and introduce themselves. You, Sam, have that kind of **strength** and so much more."

Grandpa Dan opened the teal box. It was filled with pictures of a baby in the hospital. But it wasn't like the babies Sam had seen on the diaper commercials on TV. This baby was very, very small in a plastic case, with different tubes, wires, and machines.

"Who is that Grandpa?" asked Sam. "That was you when you were born, Sam" said Grandpa Dan. "That was me?" asked Sam, very surprised. He had never seen photos of himself as a baby. "Yes," Grandpa Dan continued, "when you were born you were not strong enough to go home right away. You had to spend extra time in the hospital to gain your strength first. At the hospital, doctors and nurses helped you gain your strength by giving you special food and medicine to heal."

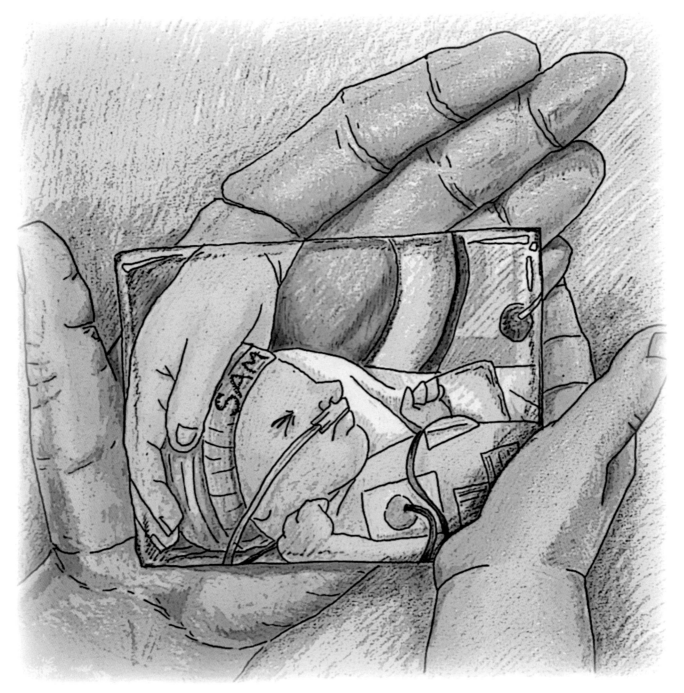

"So, what happened then?"

Sam asked, still very surprised. He had never heard this story before.

"You were in the hospital for a long time. The nurses, doctors, and the special machines gave you what you needed – food, medicine – to heal. Every day you got better, showing everyone how strong you are. Finally, all the nurses and doctors agreed that you could come home."
Grandpa Dan continued.

"As a baby, you were very **sensitive to lights, sounds, and touch**. The doctors and nurses wrapped you in tight blankets, called a swaddle, so that noise, light, and touch wouldn't bother you so much. You had so many great people helping you and even different therapists worked with you to help make your body stronger."

Sam thought for a moment. "Lights and sounds still bother me sometimes. Is this why?" Grandpa Dan looked at Sam. "Yes, and even though they can still bother you, you have improved so much since you were a baby".

"Everyday Grandma Lucy and I continue to see you grow and get stronger. We know that you have a hard time in school. It is important that you understand that the reason you have a tough time is not your fault. It is just part of what you went through as a baby and are still overcoming. It is a part of you that is not easily understood by others or even you at times, but is what makes you **a special and strong boy**."

"Wow, I really did that?" Sam could not believe he could have been strong enough to do that. "That sounds like something only heroes like Superman and Spiderman can do!" "Yes, you really did that Sam!" said Grandpa Dan.

"Your grandmother and I are so proud of you. And you are like those **Superheroes**. Remember how Spiderman lives with his Aunt and Superman lived with his adopted parents? You live with us, just like them!"

Sam hugged Grandpa Dan.

He was proud of himself for **overcoming** something like that and felt lucky to have his grandparents to help him get better.

That night as Grandpa Dan tucked him into bed, Sam thought about this story and the kids at school. He was scared and really did not want to go back to school the next day.

But he was almost seven years old now, and if Sam could be as strong as Grandpa Dan described, he can make friends with the kids in class. Sam returned to school the next day with a positive attitude.

"Today I am going to play with the other kids!".

He was so excited about what he learned last night, and how he and Superman and Spiderman had loving parents, grandparents, aunts, and uncles. He even drew a picture of his stuffed dog Hercules wearing a cape. "That is what Hercules really is", thought Sam.

"He is a superhero, like me!"

Later at aftercare Sam lined up with the other kids to get picked for teams for baseball. He waited for his name to get called once again, this time knowing he would still have fun, even if he didn't get called.

The team captains called the last name, and it wasn't Sam's. Sam looked around and noticed that this time he wasn't the only one left behind. Another student from his class, **Jimmy**, was standing next to Sam.

Jimmy had big glasses and couldn't see very far. Sam could see that Jimmy was sad he didn't get picked, just like Sam had been the day before. Sam turned to Jimmy and asked if he wanted to play another game instead of baseball.

Jimmy's face lit up as he nodded "Yes" excitedly.

The two boys walked away from the baseball field, and Sam understood that sometimes it's more fun to do something with a new friend, than to try to fit in with everyone else.

A little while after their talk, Grandpa Dan made Hercules a bright teal cape, just like in Sam's picture.

As he put the cape on Hercules, Grandpa Dan reminded Sam,

"There will always be challenges in life—but remember that you are a fighter, and you will get through them. Every day is a new chance to show the world how strong you are."

22

About the Writers

Kathryn Pearson lives in Austin, Texas where she enjoys outdoor activities like kayaking and hiking. This is Kathryn's second children's book created in collaboration with her Father, James Pearson. Kathryn is passionate about giving back to her community and supporting social organizations like To The Moon And Back. She hopes *Sam the Superhero and His Super Life* provides support and reassurance to families and their children who relate to the storyline.

James Pearson is pleased to be a part of this wonderful program for To the Moon and Back. With his magnificent daughter Kathryn, James has created stories and poems to delight, enchant, and bring a wry smile.

About the Illustrator

Lauren Jezierski grew up in Plymouth, Massachusetts and graduated both Boston University (BFA) and UMASS Dartmouth (MAE). Lauren currently teaches art in her home town at Plymouth North High School. She loves to give back to her community with murals and other art projects she creates with her students.

Lauren also helps run the Empty Bowls Community Dinner put on by the Visual and Performing Arts Department and Clay Chic to benefit the South Shore Community Action Council's Back Pack Program. Lauren lives locally with her husband and three children.

To The Moon And Back

a 501(c)3 dedicated to children born with in utero substance exposure and their families. Since 2017 To The Moon And Back has been the leader in providing support, education, and advocacy for the littlest victims of the opioid epidemic.

About the Cause

      To The Moon And Back was founded in Plymouth, MA in 2017 as a support group for families caring for children born with in utero substance exposure. Since the organization's humble beginnings, To The Moon And Back has become a leader in caring for children born with Neonatal Abstinence Syndrome (NAS) and has received multiple awards and grants for innovative programming which is now being replicated throughout the country.

Programming includes:

• Support groups for caregivers of children born with substance exposure

• Care packages for families taking substance exposed infants home from the hospital

• Annual conference for caregivers, social workers and healthcare professionals to ensure information flow as we learn to best treat and support NAS children

• Resource guides and a video series for caregivers, social workers, and health professionals

To The Moon And Back is committed to driving progress in creating the right environment and providing the right tools for children born exposed and their families need to thrive.

Made in the USA
Middletown, DE
22 September 2020